My Friend Bear

To friendship

First published 1998 by Walker Books Ltd
87 Vauxhall Walk, London SE11 5HJ

This edition published 2014

2 4 6 8 10 9 7 5 3 1

This book has been typeset in Garamond

Printed in China

British Library Cataloguing in Publication Data:
a catalogue record for this book is available from the British Library

ISBN 978-1-4063-5679-3

www.walker.co.uk

My Friend Bear

JEZ ALBOROUGH

WALKER BOOKS
AND SUBSIDIARIES
LONDON · BOSTON · SYDNEY · AUCKLAND

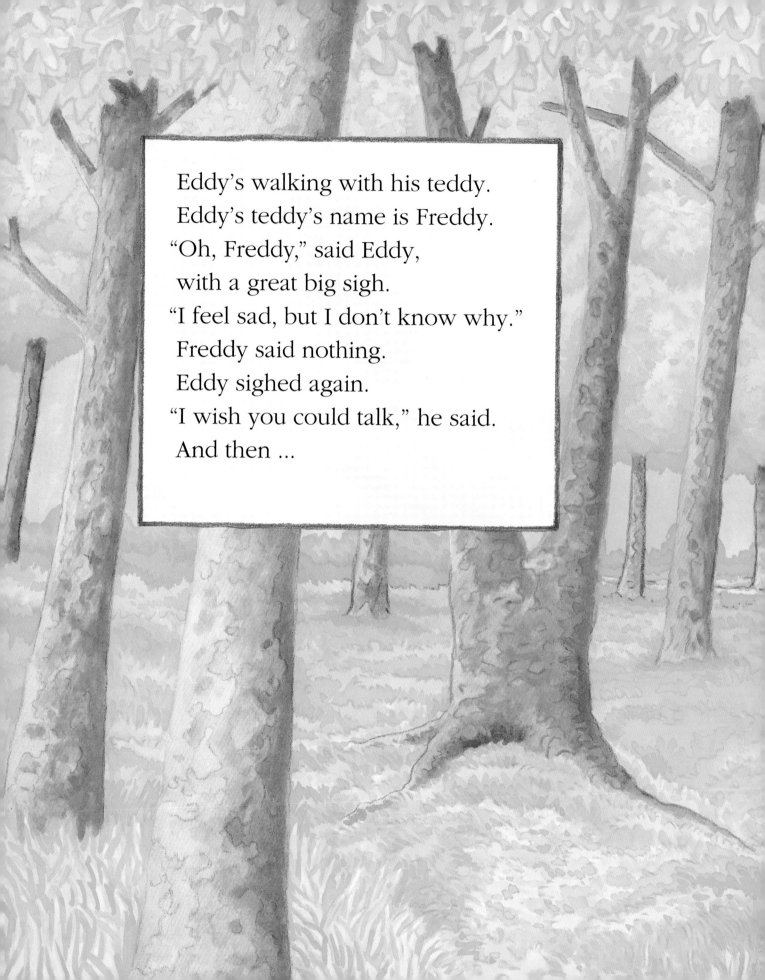

Eddy's walking with his teddy.
Eddy's teddy's name is Freddy.
"Oh, Freddy," said Eddy,
with a great big sigh.
"I feel sad, but I don't know why."
Freddy said nothing.
Eddy sighed again.
"I wish you could talk," he said.
And then ...

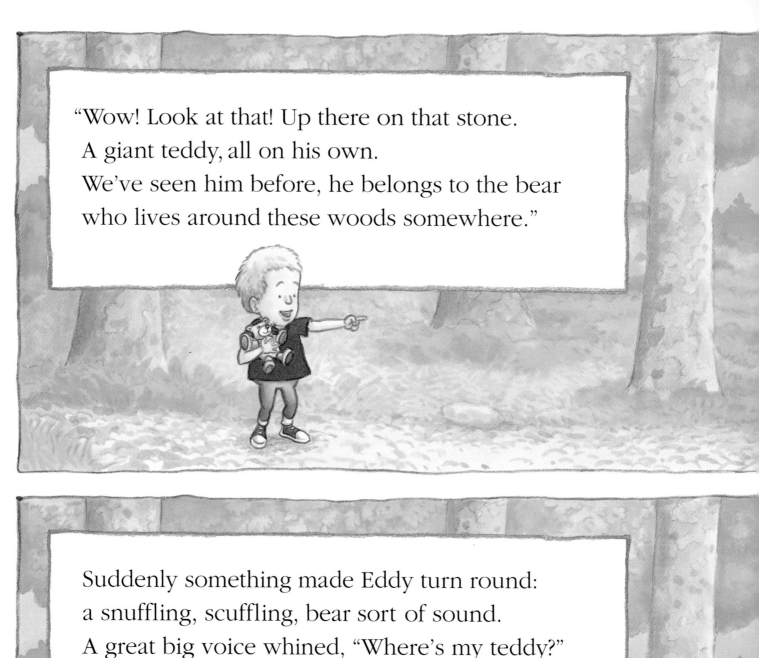

"Wow! Look at that! Up there on that stone.
A giant teddy, all on his own.
We've seen him before, he belongs to the bear
who lives around these woods somewhere."

Suddenly something made Eddy turn round:
a snuffling, scuffling, bear sort of sound.
A great big voice whined, "Where's my teddy?"
"He's coming, he's coming, let's hide!" cried Eddy.

The great big bear came shuffling by,
then stopped with a sniff and started to cry.
"Oh, teddy," he whimpered, "what can I do?
I've got no friends, apart from you.
And you can't talk, and you don't care.
I'm such a sad and lonely bear."
Then, just as he brushed a tear from his eye ...

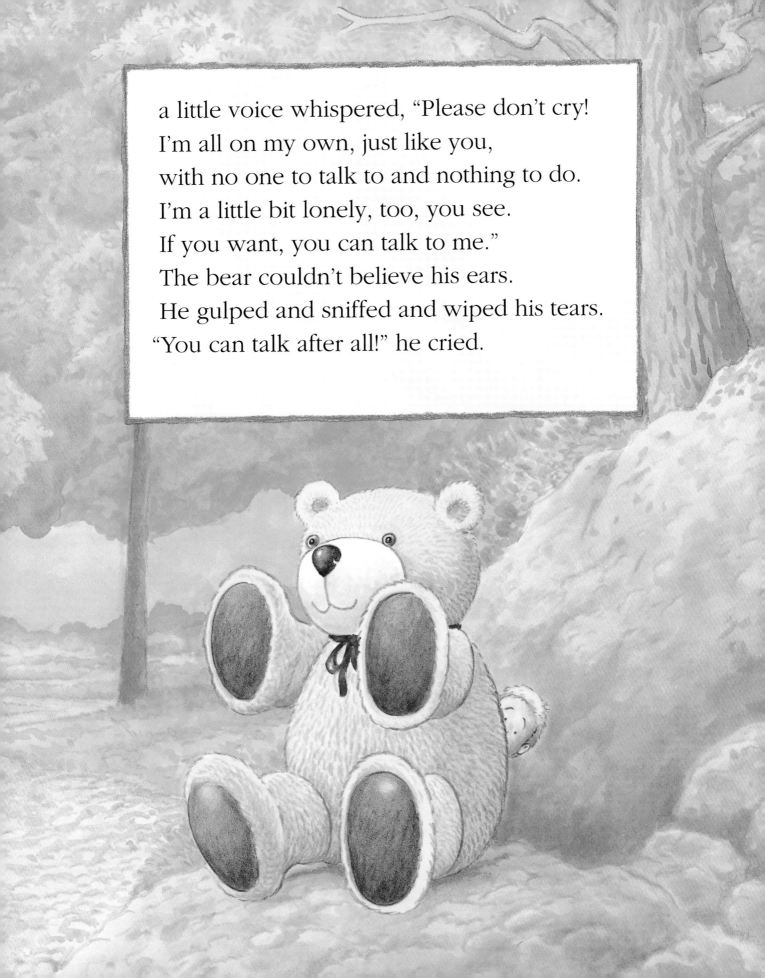

a little voice whispered, "Please don't cry!
I'm all on my own, just like you,
with no one to talk to and nothing to do.
I'm a little bit lonely, too, you see.
If you want, you can talk to me."
The bear couldn't believe his ears.
He gulped and sniffed and wiped his tears.
"You can talk after all!" he cried.

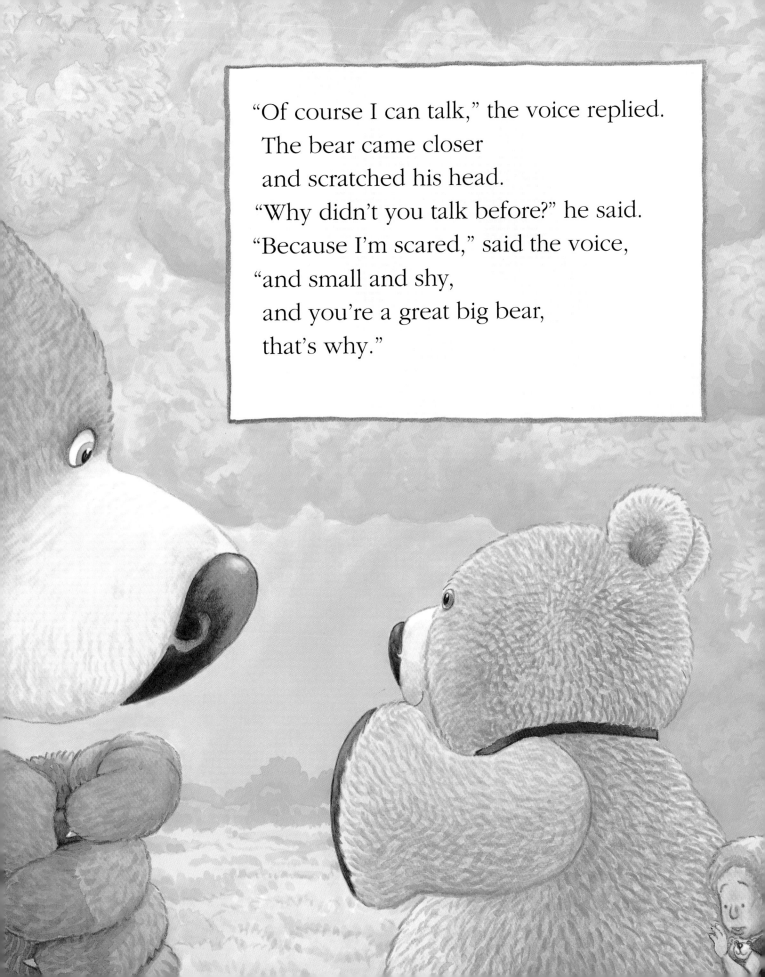

"Of course I can talk," the voice replied.
The bear came closer
and scratched his head.
"Why didn't you talk before?" he said.
"Because I'm scared," said the voice,
"and small and shy,
and you're a great big bear,
that's why."

"There, there," said the bear.
"You *are* in a muddle.
What you need
is a great big cuddle."
"No, I don't!" shrieked the voice.
"Yes, you do," said the bear.
"You just need some loving care.
Don't be scared,
you're my teddy."
"No, I'm not!" cried the voice ...

"It's me …
Eddy!"

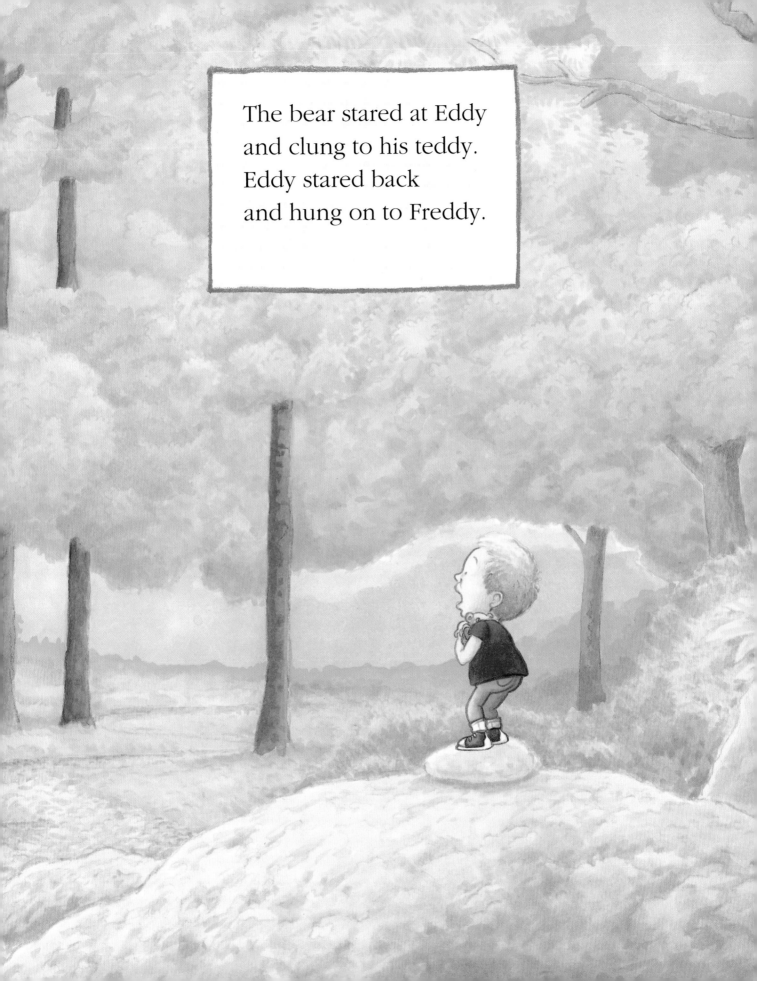

The bear stared at Eddy
and clung to his teddy.
Eddy stared back
and hung on to Freddy.

Suddenly Eddy started to grin.
He felt a chuckle rise up from within.
He tried to stop it, but it wouldn't stay down.
"What's so funny?" asked the bear, with a frown.
"It's you," giggled Eddy.
"It's you, standing there.
You're such a great big silly bear!"
"No, I'm not," said the bear.
"Yes, you are!" yelped Eddy.
"You thought you had a talking teddy."

Then the bear began to snigger.
The smile on his face grew bigger and bigger.
His great big belly wiggled and jiggled.
"I am a silly bear," he giggled.
"A talking teddy – I thought it was true,
but all along it was really you."

The bear held out his giant-sized teddy,
crouched down behind it
and said, "Hello, Eddy.
I'm a talking teddy – listen to me!
Aren't I clever? I'm only three."
Then Eddy wanted to have a go.
He held up his teddy
and squeaked, "Hello!
My name's Freddy.
How do you do?
I can talk, and
I'm only two!"

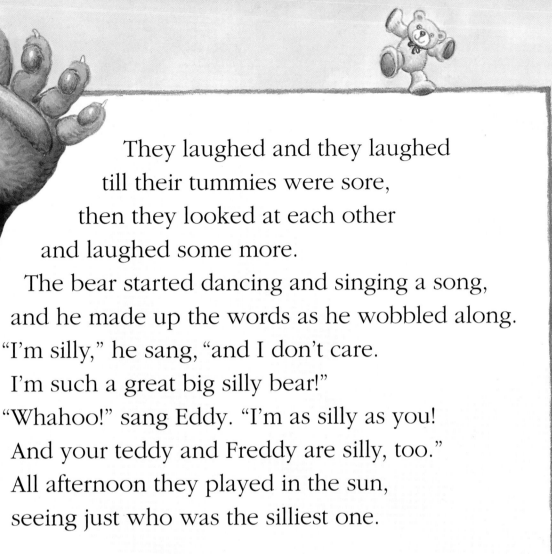

They laughed and they laughed
till their tummies were sore,
then they looked at each other
and laughed some more.
The bear started dancing and singing a song,
and he made up the words as he wobbled along.
"I'm silly," he sang, "and I don't care.
I'm such a great big silly bear!"
"Whahoo!" sang Eddy. "I'm as silly as you!
And your teddy and Freddy are silly, too."
All afternoon they played in the sun,
seeing just who was the silliest one.

When the sun began
to set in the sky,
they knew it was time
to say goodbye.

"We're friends," said Eddy.
The bear said, "Who?"
"You know," said Eddy.
"Me and you."

The bear lifted Eddy
up for a hug,
hairy and beary,
safe and snug.

"Take care," he said.
"Look after Freddy!"
"We'll come back soon,"
whispered Eddy.

Then off they walked,
with a smile and a wave.
Back to a house,
and back to a cave.
Do you think that they're lonely?
Not any more…

That's what
having friends
is for.